HARD NUTS OF HISTORY

Myths and Legends

TRACEY TURNER

ILLUSTRATED BY JAMIE LENMAN

A & C BLACK
AN IMPRINT OF BLOOMSBURY
LONDON NEW DELHI NEW YORK SYDNEY

First published 2015 by A & C Black,
an imprint of Bloomsbury Publishing Plc
50 Bedford Square, London WC1B 3DP

www.bloomsbury.com

ISBN 978-1-4729-1093-6

A CIP catalogue for this book is available from the British Library.

Printed in China by Leo Paper Products, Heshan, Guangdong

1 3 5 7 9 10 8 6 4 2

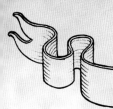
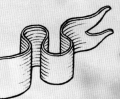

CONTENTS

INTRODUCTION

This book contains the hardest and most ruthless characters from myths and legends around the world. Some of them battled ferocious monsters, some were cunning tricksters, and some drove chariots pulled by goats. But all of them were as hard as nails.

FIND OUT ABOUT . . .

• **Hundred-headed dragons**

• **Murderous princesses**

• **Man-eating horses**

• **A head-chopping giant Green Knight**

If you've ever wanted to slay the Minotaur, chop a sea serpent's head off, or rob from the rich to give to the poor, read on. Follow the hard nuts through Sherwood Forest, into a jellyfish-infested lake, and through the darkest depths of the underworld.

As well as discovering amazing stories of monsters and mayhem, you might be in for a few surprises. Did you know, for example, that the Chinese general Hua Mulan was a woman disguised as a man? Or that Heracles murdered his own family?

You're about to meet some of the scariest hard nuts from myths and legends history . . .

Plus turn to page 14 to find out all about the Chinese Zodiac signs. Work out which Chinese year you were born in and then see if your personality matches the Chinese Zodiac description.

HERACLES

Heracles was born tough – he was strangling snakes while he was still in his cot! He's most famous for his twelve labours.

HARD NUT
RATING: 10

THE TWELVE LABOURS OF HERACLES

Hera, the Queen of the Greek gods, didn't like Heracles. She sent him mad, and he killed his family by mistake. As a punishment he had to perform twelve labours set for him by King Eurystheus – and they were quite tricky.

1. Kill the Nemean lion, a ferocious beast that could withstand all weapons. Heracles choked it with his bare hands, then wore its skin as a weapon-proof cloak.

2. Kill the Lernaean hydra, a nine-headed water snake. With each head that Heracles cut off, two more grew in its place. Heracles got help from his nephew, who burned the necks as soon as Heracles chopped off a head, so no new ones could grow.

3. Catch the Ceryneian hind, a stag with golden antlers. Catching it angered the hunting goddess, Artemis, so Heracles released it again after King Eurystheus had seen it.

4. Capture the wild boar from Mount Erymanthos. Heracles took it back to the king, who hid from it, terrified, in a giant pot.

5. Drive away the Stymphalian birds, which had bronze beaks and claws. Heracles scared them off with a pair of castanets, then shot them down with arrows.

6. Clean the Augean stables, which hadn't been cleaned in 30 years, in just one day. Heracles diverted a river to wash the stables out.

7. Capture the untameable Cretan bull. Heracles not only captured it, but rode it too.

8. Steal the man-eating horses of King Diomedes. Heracles gave them Diomedes to eat (he deserved it).

9. Fetch the girdle of the Queen of the fierce warrior women, the Amazons. Heracles had to fight to get it.

10. Capture the cattle of Geryon, a three-headed giant. Heracles managed it, despite Geryon's two-headed guard dog with a snake for its tail.

11. Bring back golden apples of the Hesperides, which were guarded by a hundred-headed dragon. Heracles swapped jobs with Atlas, so Atlas got the apples while Heracles held up the sky.

12. Fetch Cerberus, the three-headed guard-dog of the underworld. Heracles showed the hellhound to the king, then took him back.

HARDOMETER

CUNNING: 10
COURAGE: 10
SURVIVAL SKILLS: 10
RUTHLESSNESS: 10

BEOWULF

**Beowulf is a monster-battling
hero with the strength of 30 men.**

MONSTER BASHING

Beowulf, the nephew of the King of Sweden,
lived in a time when monsters plagued the land and sea,
causing death and destruction. Super-hard Beowulf
had battled sea monsters for five days and nights and
survived while he was still a child. So when he heard about
a particularly vicious monster called Grendel that was
plaguing the King of Denmark, he volunteered to go and
sort it out.

MAN-EATER

Grendel was part human, part animal, part bird, and had a
nasty habit of carrying off a sleeping guest from the King's
hall every night, and eating them.

The King was running out of warriors fast. So Beowulf stayed awake while everyone else fell asleep, and, when Grendel appeared, Beowulf was ready to fight him. Beowulf twisted off Grendel's arm, and his terrible cries woke up everyone else. They set upon Grendel together, but didn't quite manage to finish the monster off.

MONSTER MUM

Grendel's mother came for her son and took him to her underwater lair in a lake. Beowulf dived in after them, manfully fighting off swarms of poisonous jellyfish on the way. The monstrous mother had hair of writhing snakes, and a purple drooling mouth full of green fangs: she was terrifying. Beowulf chopped her in two with a magic sword, then found Grendel and chopped off his head.

BEOWULF THE HERO

Beowulf returned home to Sweden a hero, with heaps of treasure as his reward. He became king and reigned for 50 years. One day a fire-breathing dragon attacked Beowulf's hall looking for its treasure. Everyone fled in terror, apart from heroic hard nut Beowulf. He fought bravely, but was fatally wounded.

ANCIENT POEM

Beowulf's story is told in an old English epic poem, which was written between the 700s and 1100. We don't know who wrote it, but the story has survived the centuries, and it's still being translated into new versions today.

HARDOMETER

CUNNING: 10
COURAGE: 10
SURVIVAL SKILLS: 9
RUTHLESSNESS: 10

HUA MULAN

Hua Mulan is a fierce female warrior from Chinese legend, who became an army general disguised as a man.

HARD NUT RATING: 9

WARRIOR WOMAN

Even though Chinese girls weren't usually taught the same things as boys, Hua Mulan's father taught her horse-riding, archery, fencing and martial arts. When war broke out, a man from every family had to go and fight. Hua Mulan's father was too old, and her brother was too young, so Hua Mulan decided to go herself.

FEARSOME FIGHTER

Hua Mulan bought herself a horse and travelled over 16,000 kilometres to find the army. Everyone assumed she was a man, since she was dressed as one. She was just as good as the men at fighting: she fought so bravely and well that she became a general, and stayed in the army for more than ten years, until the war ended. The emperor of China was so impressed that he offered her a job, but she refused, and asked for a camel instead, which she rode back home to her family.

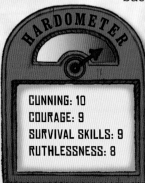

HARDOMETER

CUNNING: 10
COURAGE: 9
SURVIVAL SKILLS: 9
RUTHLESSNESS: 8

SURPRISE!

When she arrived home with some of her soldiers, still dressed as a general, no one recognised her. Her family made a feast for the visiting general, but when she sat down to eat it she dressed in women's clothes, and the secret was out.

Her soldiers were amazed to discover that their general was a woman. One of the generals who had fought with Mulan had even wanted her to marry his daughter – when he found out her secret, he wanted to marry her himself!

AN OLD STORY

The adventures of Hua Mulan are described in a poem, written down for the first time in the 500s, and rewritten many times since. When it was first written, women and men in Chinese society were supposed to stick to traditional male and female roles, so the idea of a female warrior who fooled all the men would have been much more shocking than it is now. But Hua Mulan's story is still popular (she even stars in a Disney film), and historians are still arguing over whether or not Hua Mulan was a real person.

THE CHINESE ZODIAC

Chinese years are named after an animal, which follow a 12-year cycle, always in the same order. For example, if you were born in 2006, you were born in the Year of the Dog. The year before (2005) was the Year of the Rooster and the year after (2007) was the Year of the Pig. The year 2008 was the most recent start of the 12-year cycle, the Year of the Rat.

Work out which Chinese year you were born in. Then see if your personality matches what you're supposed to be like according to the Chinese Zodiac.

Rat – Clever and successful *but* might be greedy and obstinate. Most likely to be friends with dragons, monkeys and oxen.

Ox – Honest and hardworking *but* might find it hard to communicate. Most likely to be friends with rats, snakes and roosters.

Tiger – Tolerant and brave *but* might be a bit selfish. Most likely to be friends with horses and dogs.

Rabbit – Compassionate and friendly *but* might be unwise with money and find it hard to concentrate. Most likely to be friends with goats, pigs and dogs.

Dragon – Energetic and a perfectionist, *but* might be impatient and arrogant. Most likely to be friends with rats, monkeys and roosters.

Snake – Wise and good at communicating *but* might be suspicious. Most likely to be friends with oxen and roosters.

Horse – Clever, kind and cheerful *but* might be impatient and wasteful. Most likely to be friends with goats, tigers and dogs.

Goat – Kind and sensitive, *but* might be pessimistic and moody. Most likely to be friends with rabbits, horses and pigs.

Monkey – Lively and good at solving problems, *but* might be jealous and selfish. Most likely to be friends with rats, dragons and snakes.

Rooster – Capable and warm *but* might be moody and arrogant. Most likely to be friends with dragons, oxen and snakes.

Dog – Brave, clever and faithful *but* might be critical and anxious. Most likely to be friends with tigers, rabbits and horses.

Pig – Calm, tolerant and optimistic *but* might be hot-tempered. Most likely to be friends with goats and rabbits.

THE ANIMAL RACE

Different stories explain the order of the animals. In one of them, the Jade Emperor says he's going to name the years after the animals in the order they arrive at his palace. The animals have to cross a river, but the rat and the cat can't swim, and hitch a lift on the ox. Just before they reach the shore, the rat pushes the cat in the water, and runs ahead to become the first (and that's why there's no Year of the Cat).

ANANSI

Anansi is the trickster god of West African and Caribbean myths. He's a spider – unusual for a hard nut hero – but what he lacks in strength he makes up for in cleverness and cunning.

HARD NUT RATING: 7.5

SPIDER MAN

There are lots of different stories about Anansi, and lots of different versions of each one. Anansi isn't always a spider – sometimes he's a man, but with eight eyes or eight legs. The tale of how he came by his stories in the first place shows his talent for trickery.

TRICKING THE PYTHON

The sky god, Nyame, had all the stories in the world. Anansi asked how much they would cost to buy, and Nyame replied that Anansi had to bring him Onini the python, Osebo the leopard, Mmoatia the dwarf, and the Mmoboro hornets. First Anansi went to the python, and wondered aloud whether the python was really longer than a palm branch or not. Onini said that he was, and agreed to be tied to the branch so he could be measured accurately – Anansi had tricked him, tied him to the branch, and took the helpless snake to Nyame.

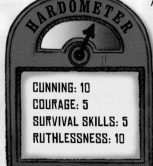

HARDOMETER

CUNNING: 10
COURAGE: 5
SURVIVAL SKILLS: 5
RUTHLESSNESS: 10

MORE TRICKERY

Anansi dug a trap for the leopard, Osebo. When Osebo fell in, Anansi offered to help him out by spinning a web. As soon as he had the leopard trapped in his web, he took him to Nyame. Next, Anansi persuaded the hornets to get inside a container to shelter from the rain (even though it wasn't raining), and captured them as well. And finally, he got Mmoatia the dwarf to hit a doll he'd covered with sticky gum so that Mmoatia was then stuck to the doll. Now he'd caught everyone Nyame had asked for, and Nyame made Anansi the god of all stories.

SMALL AND MIGHTY

Stories about Anansi are some of the best known in West Africa. They've been told for centuries, but weren't written down until a hundred or so years ago. Many of them show how a small, apparently powerless character can defeat much bigger opponents, so it's not surprising they were popular with the people brought from West Africa to the Caribbean as part of the terrible trade in African slaves.

AENEAS

Aeneas is the legendary heroic, handsome ancestor of the ancient Romans.

HARD NUT
RATING: 7.3

DESTINY QUEST

Aeneas's father, Anchises, was a member of the royal household of Troy. His mother was even more impressive: she was Venus, the goddess of love and beauty. Aeneas fought heroically in the Trojan War, between the Greeks and the Trojans. When the Greeks won, Aeneas set off in search of his prophesied destiny to found a new city, carrying his lame father from the burning city of Troy, and leading a band of loyal Trojans.

WANDERINGS

After wandering about for a few years, attacked by plague and the horrible bird-women, the harpies (see page 54), Aeneas arrived in Carthage, where Queen Dido fell in love with him. After a year, the gods reminded Aeneas that he should be founding a new city, so he left. Dido was so heartbroken that she stabbed herself and died, cursing the descendants of Aeneas and promising that Carthage would forever be at war with them.

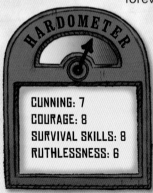

HARDOMETER

CUNNING: 7
COURAGE: 8
SURVIVAL SKILLS: 8
RUTHLESSNESS: 6

THE UNDERWORLD

In Italy, Aeneas went to the underworld to meet his father, Anchises, who'd died on their travels. Anchises showed Aeneas his future descendants, who included the twins Romulus and Remus – Romulus was the legendary founder of the city of Rome.

BIG PIG

When he finally arrived in Italy, Aeneas spotted an enormous sow lying by the banks of a river (which turned out to be the River Tiber) with a litter of 30 piglets. The prophecy had described the pigs, so Aeneas knew he must have arrived at his destination. Of course, things weren't that easy – first he had to fight his future wife's boyfriend, but with the help of the local friendly Etruscan people, Aeneas founded the city of Lavinium, named after his wife Lavinia.

ANCIENT ROMAN HERO

The ancient Romans were keen on having a heroic Trojan ancestor for the founder of the city of Rome. The Roman writer, Virgil, wrote a long poem all about Aeneas (called *The Aeneid*) that was very popular with the ancient Romans.

CÚ CHULAINN

Cú Chulainn is the son of the god Lugh, a superhuman warrior hero in Irish myth.

HARD NUT
RATING: 8.3

GUARDING CHULAINN

Cú Chulainn means 'Chulainn's hound'. He got his name when he was a child, after he killed a guard dog that belonged to a blacksmith called Chulainn in self-defence (he was a tough little boy). Cú Chulainn offered to train a new guard dog, and while it was growing up he'd take on guard dog duties for Chulainn himself.

WARRIOR TRAINING

A Scottish warrior woman called Scathach trained Cú Chulainn to fight, and Cú Chulainn became one of the best warriors ever. He was so fearsome and deadly because of his battle frenzy, which changed him from an ordinary man into a kind of monster in the heat of battle – his hair stood on end, his muscles swelled, one eye stuck out while the other sank back, and he howled and breathed fire – enough to terrify anyone. He also had the advantage of some magic weapons: a spear that always killed, never wounded, and a chariot that could become invisible.

BROWN BULL

Queen Medb of Connacht wanted the famous Brown Bull of Cooley, but the people of Ulster wouldn't sell it to her. So she decided to invade and take it from them – and to make things easier for her, a curse made all the men of Ulster take to their beds sick. Cú Chulainn, though, wasn't an Ulsterman. Single-handedly, he fought each one of the Connacht champions and defeated them all.

THE END OF CÚ CHULAINN

Queen Medb plotted revenge, and Cú Chulainn was finally killed with a magic spear by a warrior called Lugaid. Cú Chulainn tied himself to a standing stone so he could die with dignity. When Lugaid was sure Cú Chulainn was dead, he went to cut his head off, but – even though he was dead – Cú Chulainn still managed to chop off Lugaid's hand. Cú Chulainn died young, fulfilling the prophesy that he would have a glorious life, but a short one.

HARDOMETER

CUNNING: 8
COURAGE: 9
SURVIVAL SKILLS: 7
RUTHLESSNESS: 9

THOR

When the Vikings heard thunder, they believed it to be Thor, the god of Thunder, rampaging across the sky in his chariot.

HARD NUT
RATING: 9.3

LIGHTNING GOD

Thor was enormous, with a huge red beard and fierce, burning eyes. His role was to protect Asgard, the land of the gods, from attack by giants. His main weapon in the fight against the giants was a magical hammer called Mjolnir, which returned to him when he threw it and created bolts of lightning. He wore a magic belt that doubled his strength, and rode in a mighty chariot pulled by two especially fierce goats called Tooth-grinder and Tooth-gnasher.

GIANT BASHING

There are lots of stories about Thor's giant-killing exploits. In one story, Thor was on his way to fight the greatest giant of all, Hrungnir. So the giants created a mist calf – a giant bull made with clay and the heart of a horse – to scare him. But the sight of the god in his chariot pulled by the fearsome goats, and with thunder and lightning crashing around him, terrified the bull, and it was chopped to pieces by Thor's servant. When he met Hrungnir, Thor's hammer flew through the sky and smashed Hrungnir's weapon to pieces. Hrungnir died, but unfortunately fell on top of Thor as he dropped dead. Even more unfortunately,

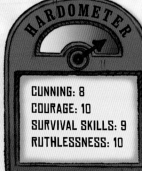

HARDOMETER

CUNNING: 8
COURAGE: 10
SURVIVAL SKILLS: 9
RUTHLESSNESS: 10

a piece of Hrungnir's weapon lodged in Thor's head, and stayed there forever. Thor was trapped underneath his giant enemy, and had to be rescued by his son.

THOR'S STOLEN HAMMER

In another story, Thor's hammer was stolen by the giants. The giants promised to return it if the giant Thrym could marry the goddess Freya. So Thor disguised himself as Freya, dressed in a bridal gown. At the wedding, Thor aroused suspicion by stuffing himself with a whole ox, eight salmon and three barrels of wine. But Thor got away with his disguise: the giants brought out the hammer to bless the wedding, and Thor leapt forward, grabbed it and killed all the giants with it.

THE NINE NORSE WORLDS

In Viking mythology there are nine worlds, populated by giants, dwarves, elves, human beings (living and dead), gods and goddesses.

Asgard – The land of the gods known as Aesir (male gods) and Asynjur (goddesses), ruled by Odin, king of the gods, and Frigg, queen of the gods. Half of all Viking warriors killed in battle end up in Valhalla, inside the gates of Asgard, fighting by day and feasting by night. The other half go to the goddess Freya.

Vanaheim – The land of the Vanir gods – a race of older gods. No one knows where it is.

Alfheim – The land of the light elves, ruled by the god Freyr. The light elves are magical creatures who might help or hinder humans.

Svartalfheim – Land of the Sun-hating dark elves, who make trouble for humans.

Nidavellir – Land of the dwarves. They live underground and are excellent blacksmiths.

Jotunheim – Land of the giants, who are deadly enemies of the Aesir gods.

Midgard – The land where people live – the Earth we know. Midgard is connected to Asgard by a rainbow bridge.

Muspelheim – Land of fire, ruled by the giant Surt.

Niflheim – Land of mists, the coldest and darkest of the worlds. Helheim, the land of the dead, is in Niflheim.

ASGARD

ALFHEIM

VANAHEIM

NIDAVELLIR

MIDGARD

SVARTALFHEIM

JOTUNHEIM

MUSPELHEIM

NIFLHEIM

DURGA

Durga is a powerful, lion-riding, many-armed warrior goddess from the Hindu religion.

BUFFALO DEMON

Mahisa the buffalo demon was indestructible, and went on the rampage, killing people and attacking the land of the gods. His war with the gods continued for a hundred years, and eventually Mahisa won and became ruler of the gods. Lord Brahma, the creator of the Universe, Lord Vishnu, its maintainer, and Lord Shiva, the destroyer of the Universe, decided to get together and do something about Mahisa. They created Durga.

UNIVERSE-SHAKING

Lord Vishnu gave Durga ten arms, Lord Brahma gave the goddess her feet, and other gods gave her qualities and objects that made her unbeatable, including golden armour, three eyes, and a lion to ride. Durga could make the seas boil, crumble continents, raise mountains, and her roar was so loud it shook the Universe.

DEFEATING THE DEMON

Durga gathered an army to fight Mahisa. If her soldiers were defeated, she breathed new life into them and they fought again. Her army won. Furious, Mahisa turned himself into a buffalo and charged at Durga's army. Durga's lion attacked and fought him, while Durga lassoed him. The demon changed shape and became a lion; Durga cut off his head. He became a man and she stabbed him. Then he turned into an elephant and she got the better of him again. He turned back into a buffalo and threw mountains at Durga, but she pinned him down then killed him with her trident, finally defeating him.

DURGA'S FESTIVAL

Every year, Hindus all over the world celebrate a ten-day festival in Durga's honour, marking her defeat of the buffalo demon, a triumph of good over evil. A statue of Durga stands throughout the festival, until it's immersed in water, to symbolise Durga going home to Lord Shiva, her husband, after her victory.

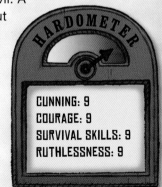

HARDOMETER

CUNNING: 9
COURAGE: 9
SURVIVAL SKILLS: 9
RUTHLESSNESS: 9

QUETZALCOATL

Quetzalcoatl is a feathered-snake god worshipped in Mexico and Central America for centuries.

HARD NUT RATING: 5

BIRD-SNAKE-MAN

Quetzalcoatl is a combination of a quetzal bird, a brightly coloured bird that lives in Central America, and a snake, but he's also sometimes shown as a man, with a tall crown and a shell necklace. He was originally a god of vegetation, connected to the rain god, but became god of the morning and evening star, and a symbol of dying and being born again.

AZTEC CREATOR

In Aztec mythology, one world existed after another. The Aztec world was the fifth world. Quetzalcoatl made the human race after going into the underworld to bring back bones from previous unsuccessful versions of humans. He was chased out by the Death Lord, and dropped the bones, which shattered. The Earth goddess then ground them into flour, and Quetzalcoatl mixed the flour with his own blood, and brought new humans to life. After that he protected and helped humans. He stole grain from the red ants and showed humans how to grow maize, and also introduced books, calendars, astronomy and crafts.

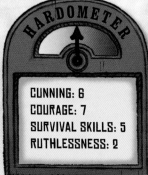

HARDOMETER

CUNNING: 6
COURAGE: 7
SURVIVAL SKILLS: 5
RUTHLESSNESS: 2

HORRIBLE REFLECTION

The god Tezcatlipoca wanted people to make human sacrifices. According to one version of the story, Tezcatlipoca got Quetzalcoatl drunk and showed him his awful reflection. Horrified, Quetzalcoatl threw himself onto a burning pyre, from which birds flew out, and his heart ascended to heaven and became the morning and evening star. In another version of the story, he sailed off on a raft made of serpents. It was said he would return when his people were in danger.

CONQUERING QUETZALCOATL

The Aztecs thought that the Spanish conqueror, Hernàn Cortés, was the god Quetzalcoatl come back to save them. They couldn't have been more wrong – Cortés conquered them, destroyed their beautiful capital city, and enslaved or killed most of the Aztecs.

FINN MCCOOL

Finn McCool is the legendary leader of a tough Irish warrior band, and also a giant who stomped across the sea from Ireland to Scotland.

HARD NUT
RATING: 8.8

CLEVER FISH

McCool was brought up by a warrior woman and taught to fight and hunt. When he was still a child he met a druid who'd spent years trying to catch the Salmon of Knowledge. He'd finally caught the salmon and was roasting it when McCool touched the fish, burnt his thumb, and put it in his mouth to cool it – he gained the fish's knowledge as a result, which would come in handy later.

WARRIOR BAND

The toughest group of warriors in Ireland, the Fianna, was led by Goll MacMorna. Every Halloween, a fire-breathing fairy called Allain enchanted the men of Tara, where the King of Ireland lived, and sent them to sleep with his music, before burning down the palace. Goll MacMorna and the Fianna couldn't stop the fairy, but Finn McCool could. Armed with his magical weapons, McCool kept himself awake by sticking his spear into his forehead. Then he killed Allain with his spear. After that, MacMorna stepped aside and Finn McCool became the leader of the Fianna.

HARDOMETER

CUNNING: 10
COURAGE: 8
SURVIVAL SKILLS: 9
RUTHLESSNESS: 8

GIANT MCCOOL

In some stories, Finn McCool is a giant. In one, the giant Benandonner came stomping across the causeway from Scotland to Ireland. McCool set out to meet him, but realised that Benandonner was far bigger than him so he and his wife hatched a plan. When Benandonner turned up, McCool's wife Oonagh pretended that McCool, wrapped up like a baby, was McCool's child. She said McCool would be back soon and offered Benandonner one of her cakes, in which she'd hidden a chunk of iron – the giant broke his teeth, but watched in amazement as the baby ate the cakes without a problem. He left before the 'real' McCool came home.

MCCOOL'S CAUSEWAY

The Giant's Causeway – thousands of interlocking columns on the coast of Northern Ireland – is supposed to be the stepping stones Finn McCool used to walk to Scotland without getting his feet wet. There are lots more stories about Finn McCool, both as a warrior and as a giant.

MEDEA

Medea is a princess you wouldn't want to mess with. She has magical powers and ruthless cunning.

HARD NUT
RATING: 9.5

GOLDEN FLEECE

Medea was the daughter of the King of Colchis, land of the golden fleece. One day, the Greek hero Jason arrived, in search of the fleece. The King of Colchis set Jason an impossible task in return for the fleece: to plough a field using two massive fire-breathing bulls, and sow it with dragon's teeth. Medea fell instantly in love with the handsome hero, and gave Jason a magic potion to protect him from the bulls. Then she told him how to deal with the ferocious warriors that sprouted from

NOW YOU TRY.

the dragon's teeth. When the King didn't keep his word, Medea drugged the dragon that guarded the fleece, helped Jason steal it, and they set sail together. To slow down her father, who was in hot pursuit, she killed her little brother and dropped bits of him over the side of the ship, so that her father would stop to pick up his body.

MORE BODY BITS

Medea and Jason fled to Iolchus, where Jason was the rightful king, but was ruled by King Pelias. Medea thought of a way of getting rid of Pelias: she fooled his daughters into performing a gruesome spell. She showed them an old ram, which she chopped up and threw into a cauldron, and magically restored it to a young lamb. Pelias's daughters tried to work the same magic on their father, but only succeeded in chopping him to bits.

MURDEROUS MEDEA

Medea and Jason ran away to Corinth, where they had two sons. But then Jason made the terrible mistake of dumping Medea so he could marry the King of Corinth's daughter. In revenge, Medea killed Jason's new bride by giving her a poisoned cloak, then killed her own sons – just to upset Jason even more – and ran away. She ended up marrying Aegeus, King of Athens, but was banished after she tried to kill his son, Theseus (see page 52). Eventually, Medea became immortal, and married the Greek hero Achilles in the afterlife.

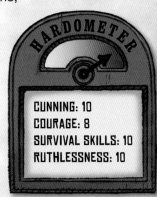

HARDOMETER

CUNNING: 10
COURAGE: 8
SURVIVAL SKILLS: 10
RUTHLESSNESS: 10

FUMO LIYONGO

Fumo Liyongo was actually a real person, a Swahili poet from East Africa, who lived some time between the 1300s and 1600s. But the real person has become mixed up with his legendary character, who is twice as fast and tall as any man, strong as a lion, a deadly accurate archer, and terrifying to look at.

HARD NUT RATING: 6.5

SIBLING RIVALRY

Fumo Liyongo's poem tells the story of his struggle with his brother, Mringwari, who was Sultan of Pate but worried about Liyongo's claim to his throne, because he was so much better qualified for the job. Mringwari tried to get rid of Liyongo in various different ways. First he sent him off to get married to a beautiful woman a long way away. Then once he was settled, Mringwari tried to have him murdered but Liyongo outwitted the killers.

ESCAPE FROM PRISON

Next Mringwari lured Liyongo to Pate, where he threw him in prison. Liyongo was told he had three days before his execution, but he was granted a last wish. Liyongo asked for a special dance called a gungu to be held where he could see it. Then he made up a poem, which he sang to the servant girl who brought his food, asking his mother to send him a cake with tools hidden inside it, to cut his chains. The servant girl sang the poem to Liyongo's mother, and she did as she was asked. The wild dancing of the gunga drowned out the noise of Liyongo setting himself free with the tools hidden in the cake, and he killed the guards and escaped in the confusion.

LIYONGO'S LAST STAND

Mringwari promised Liyongo's treacherous son his daughter in marriage if he helped kill Liyongo. The son discovered the secret of Liyongo's resistance to weapons: only a copper dagger driven through his navel could kill him. He waited until his father was asleep, then stabbed him through the navel with the dagger, and ran away. Mortally wounded, Liyongo armed himself, and knelt by the village well for three days. After three days, the people of the village realised that the hard nut Liyongo was actually dead, but too tough to lie down.

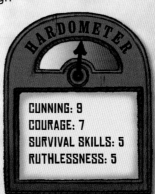

HARDOMETER

CUNNING: 9
COURAGE: 7
SURVIVAL SKILLS: 5
RUTHLESSNESS: 5

AFRICAN CREATION MYTHS

Africa is a vast continent with a wide range of different people, different languages, and different myths and legends. All cultures have creation myths – stories that explain how the world and human beings began. Below are two versions of creation myths from different parts of Africa.

KINTU: FROM UGANDA

This story explains why there's sickness and death on Earth.

Kintu was the only man in the world, living alone with his cattle. The god who'd created the world, Ggulu, lived in heaven with his children, who would sometimes go down to Earth to play.

One day while they were spending time on Earth, the goddess Nambi met Kintu and fell in love with him. They decided to get married, and went back to heaven to ask her father's permission. He wasn't keen on the idea, but reluctantly agreed, and sent Nambi and Kintu back to Earth, warning them not to tell Nambi's brother Walumbe. Ggulu was worried that Walumbe (meaning 'causing sickness and death') would want to go with them.

On the way back to Earth, Nambi realised she'd forgotten the grain for her chickens. Despite Kintu's pleas, she went back to get it – and, sure enough, she met Walumbe on the way. Walumbe followed her back to Kintu, and brought suffering, disease and death with him.

MBOMBO: FROM THE KUBA PEOPLE (PART OF MODERN-DAY DEMOCRATIC REPUBLIC OF CONGO)

The god Mbombo lived in a dark world filled with water. He felt sick, and vomited the Sun, Moon and stars. The Sun evaporated some of the water, and clouds formed and land rose above the water.

Mbombo vomited again, bringing up nine animals – the leopard, the eagle, the crocodile, the fish, the tortoise, a black big cat like a puma, a white heron, a scarab and a goat. He also vomited lots of people.

The animals created all other animals, except white ants, created by Mbombo's son, who died creating them; the kite, created by another of Mbombo's sons; and plants, created by yet another son.

The black big cat caused trouble, so Mbombo sent it to live in the sky as a thunderbolt. This left the people without fire, so Mbombo taught them how to make it. Then he went up to live in heaven, leaving one of the men to become the first ruler of the Kuba people.

CLEVER COYOTE

Native American Indian myths tell stories of Clever Coyote, who's not the strongest, but often the cleverest.

HARD NUT RATING: 8.3

COYOTE-MAN

Coyotes are wild dogs similar to wolves, and Clever Coyote shares their cunning and voracious appetite. In stories he isn't always a coyote, but sometimes a man, and can also shape-shift into other creatures.

MONSTER SLAYING

There are lots of stories about Clever Coyote. One of them is about a monster that had eaten all the fish, fruit, and animals, so that there was nothing left for the people to eat. They called on Coyote for help. He took a long rope, some wood and something to make a spark for a fire. Then Coyote stood on a hill and called the monster names. Eventually, unimpressed but quite cross, the monster came and ate him. Inside the monster Coyote quickly built a fire. Each time the monster opened his mouth, trying to blow the fire out, Coyote threw something out: each fish, fruit and animal the monster had eaten, one by one. Coyote escaped as the monster gave his last gasp.

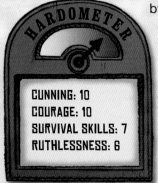

HARDOMETER

CUNNING: 10
COURAGE: 10
SURVIVAL SKILLS: 7
RUTHLESSNESS: 6

THE MONSTER AND THE BUFFALO

In another story a monster had stolen all the buffalo.
The people didn't want to kill the monster, because his
companion was a little boy, who tends the buffalo. Coyote
has the idea of sending the boy pets that might be able
to free the buffalo – they send a mouse, then a bird, but
the monster sends them both away. Finally Coyote goes
himself – the boy loves him but the monster threatens
to eat them both. When the boy cries, Coyote howls to
comfort him – and his howls make the buffalo nervous and
stampede away. The people kill the monster, and the boy
goes to live with them, happily ever after.

COYOTE STORIES

As well as tricking monsters, Coyote was also involved in
lots of other stories, some about the creation of the world.
He's a slippery character: in some stories, he's not clever
and cunning, but a figure of fun who gets things wrong.

GILGAMESH

The story of Gilgamesh, the hard nut King of Uruk, is one of the oldest stories ever written down, from one of the oldest civilizations on Earth.

HARD NUT RATING: 7.5

TYRANT KING

Gilgamesh's story is probably based on a real king of Mesopotamia (the area that's now Iraq). In the story his mother was a goddess, and his father was a man who became a god. Gilgamesh was King of Uruk, the world's strongest man as well as its greatest king, and ruled for 126 years. But he wasn't all good: he was also a bit of a tyrant, and his people asked the gods to do something about him. The gods created a wild man called Enkidu to fight Gilgamesh. Gilgamesh won the fight, but only just, and the two hard nuts became best mates.

GILGAMESH AND ENKIDU

Together, the two pals killed lions, wrestled a sacred bull, and generally proved themselves to be as hard as nails. They fought Huwawa, the terrifying, fire-breathing giant of the Cedar Forest, and Gilgamesh managed to capture him. Enkidu chopped off the monster's head, but was cursed as a result. With the monster dead, Gilgamesh and Enkidu were free to collect timber from the forest to build a city gate for Uruk.

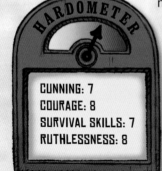

HARDOMETER

CUNNING: 7
COURAGE: 8
SURVIVAL SKILLS: 7
RUTHLESSNESS: 8

GILGAMESH IN THE UNDERWORLD

When Enkidu died, Gilgamesh was grief-stricken. After Enkidu's burial, Gilgamesh decided to travel to the underworld, to find answers to questions about his own death, and the meaning of life. On the way to the end of the world, he met lions and hideous scorpion-men who guarded the Sun. In the underworld, Gilgamesh was challenged to stay awake for six days and seven nights, in return for immortality. But he fell asleep. Realising he was a mortal man who would die, Gilgamesh returned to Uruk, and wrote his stories on the gates of the city. When he died, the Euphrates River parted, and Gilgamesh was buried at the bottom.

EPIC POEM

The earliest version of the *Epic of Gilgamesh* was written on clay tablets nearly 5,000 years ago. It's one of the oldest surviving written stories in the world.

THUGINE

Thugine is the water-dwelling rainbow serpent of Australian Aboriginal mythology, whose arched back makes a rainbow.

HARD NUT
RATING: 8.3

CREATING THE WORLD

An Aboriginal story describes how Thugine created the world. During the Dreaming – the time before the world we know now – the world was flat and bare. Thugine came out from underneath the ground and gave birth to all the animals of the world. She made the mountains and spilled water over them to make rivers and lakes and the sea. She also made the Sun, fire and all the colours of the rainbow.

THUGINE'S LAWS

The Rainbow Serpent made laws, and said that those who followed her laws would become human; those who didn't would be turned to stone. She gave each tribe of humans an animal symbol to identify them. The people weren't allowed to eat the animal that was their group's symbol, and that way there was enough food for everyone. The tribes lived happily, knowing their land would never be taken from them (though sadly it was – when the Europeans arrived in Australia).

THE WANDERING BOYS

Even though Thugine created the Earth and provided for humans, people feared her and she lurked in water. In one story a tribe of hunters was camping close to a beach. When everyone went out to fish and hunt, two boys stayed behind to guard the camp. They were warned about Thugine, but it was so hot they decided to walk to the beach, where they could hear great waves breaking. When they got to the palm-fringed beach, the water looked so cool and inviting, that they played in the breaking waves. Thugine rushed to the edge of the sea and grabbed them. When the hunters returned, they looked for the boys. When they saw two dark rocks jutting out of the sea, they knew what had happened.

WANDERING ROCKS

The Wandering Boys' rocks are still in the sea, between Double Island Point and Inskip Point in Queensland, Australia. When there's a rainbow in the sky, people tell the story of the Wandering Boys, captured and turned to stone by the Rainbow Serpent.

HARDOMETER

CUNNING: 8
COURAGE: 8
SURVIVAL SKILLS: 9
RUTHLESSNESS: 8

THE MONKEY KING

The Monkey King of Chinese legend, also known as Sun Wu Kong, hatched from a stone egg to become ruler on the island of the monkeys.

HARD NUT RATING: 8.3

MONKEY'S TRICKS

Monkey's story comes from a novel written in the 1500s. The Monkey King became one of the world's most powerful rulers. His weapon was a magic staff, which could transform from the size of a needle to an enormous weapon weighing several tonnes, and could fight for its master on its own. Monkey could also cover thousands of miles in one jump (with the aid of his cloud-walking boots), transform into different creatures, freeze demons, gods and humans, and change his hairs into weapons, or even clones of himself.

IMMORTAL MONKEY

When Hell tried to collect his soul, the Monkey King should have been reincarnated (like all other living things), but instead he deleted his name from the list of the dead so that he would never die. The Jade Emperor, ruler of the Universe, didn't like Monkey's tricks, so he brought him to heaven to look after the Cloud Horses. Monkey was furious at his lowly job, and caused so much trouble that the Jade Emperor gave him the title Great Sage, Equal of Heaven, and hoped he would stop annoying everyone.

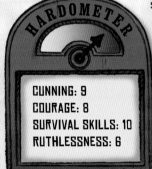

HARDOMETER

CUNNING: 9
COURAGE: 8
SURVIVAL SKILLS: 10
RUTHLESSNESS: 6

MONKEY THE THIEF

Monkey ate peaches and drank a special eternal-life potion that he'd stolen from the gods. The gods chased him back to Earth, where he put up a fierce fight with the help of the other monkeys. To try and stop Monkey causing trouble, the gods sent for Buddha. He offered the Monkey King a challenge: to jump out of his hand. Monkey jumped a huge distance, and thought he'd jumped to the edge of the world, but he hadn't made it past the tips of Buddha's fingers.

MONKEY IN HEAVEN

Monkey was imprisoned in a mountain for 500 years. When he was released, he was much less troublesome. He travelled with a monk on a quest to find the Buddha's holy writings, facing terrible monsters on the way, which he defeated using his special powers. Now that he'd changed his ways, Monkey was eventually allowed into Heaven.

RE

Re is the ancient Egyptian god of the Sun, the most powerful of all the gods and creator of everything.

ANCIENT TEMPLES

The ancient Egyptians built lots of temples in Re's honour, which were open to the sky because Re was supposed to be present when the Sun shone. The Egyptians drew Re as a man with the head of a bird and the golden Sun on his head, carrying a sceptre in one hand and an ankh in the other – a cross with a looped top that was the symbol of life. The ankh was so special to the Egyptians that only kings were allowed to carry them.

RE'S CREATION

According to the Egyptians, Re created the world and all the other gods. Re lived before time began in the form of a snake. He created all the gods – he sneezed out Shu, the god of air, spat out Tefnut, goddess of moisture. Shu and Tefnut had children, Geb (the Earth) and Nut (the sky), who had children themselves. Re sent Shu and Tefnut out across the sea and made an island for himself, where he created all the animals, birds and plants, calling their names as each one formed. He created human beings from his tears.

TRICKERY

The goddess Isis tricked Re into telling her his secret name: she took some of his spit, mixed it with clay and made it into a snake, which bit Re. He became ill, and Isis offered to cure him if he would tell her his secret name. Isis passed the secret on to her son, Horus and the secret gave them both power.

NIGHT AND DAY

The sky goddess Nut swallowed Re, the Sun, each night and gave birth to him again each morning. During the daytime, Re sailed through the sky in his special boat, with the gods Seth and Mehen. At night time they travelled through the underworld and fought off demons. Re's enemy, Apophis, the serpent, led the attacks. Seth would stab Apophis each night with his spear. The ancient Egyptians believed that if this didn't happen, the Sun wouldn't rise in the morning.

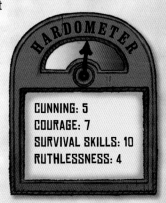

HARDOMETER

CUNNING: 5
COURAGE: 7
SURVIVAL SKILLS: 10
RUTHLESSNESS: 4

ANCIENT EGYPTIAN GODS

The Ancient Egyptians worshipped hundreds of different gods. These are some of the most important ones.

Re: I'm god of the Sun and creation and top god. Every night, Nut swallows me, and I'm reborn every morning.

Nut: I'm the sky goddess, wife and sister of Geb, and mother of Osiris, Isis, Seth and Nephthys.

Geb: I'm the Earth god, husband and brother of Nut, and father of her children.

Osiris: I was once king of the gods, but I was murdered by my jealous brother, Seth. Now I'm king of the underworld instead.

Isis: I'm Osiris's wife and sister, mother of Horus, and goddess of motherhood and children. I mourn the dead and protect coffins – because of my murdered husband.

Seth: I'm Osiris's brother, and also his murderer. I'm the god of violence and thunderstorms.

Nephthys: I'm Seth, Osiris and Isis' sister, and wife of Seth. I protect the dead, and I'm the mother of Anubis.

Horus: I'm Osiris' and Isis' son. I'm the sky god – that's why I've got a falcon's head.

Anubis: I'm Seth and Nephthys' son. I guide the dead through the underworld. Jackals used to haunt ancient Egyptian graveyards – that's why I look like this. I helped embalm Osiris after Seth killed him.

Bastet: I'm the cat goddess and goddess of women and children.

Thoth: Sometimes I have an ibis's head, and sometimes a baboon's, depending on my mood. I'm god of writing and wisdom, and I helped Isis bring Osiris back from the dead.

49

ROBIN HOOD

Robin Hood is the legendary leader of his band of merry men – a group of outlaws who lived in Sherwood Forest in Nottinghamshire, England. Handy with a bow and arrow, he famously stole from the rich to give to the poor.

ENEMY OF INJUSTICE

Some of the first stories about Robin Hood show him as a peasant resisting unjust officials, including Robin Hood's worst enemy, the Sheriff of Nottingham. More recent stories suggest Robin Hood was a lord who'd been robbed of his birthright.

COME DINE WITH ROBIN HOOD

There are lots of stories about Robin Hood, and many of them show him and his merry men robbing rich people and sharing the money they stole among the poor. Robin Hood would 'invite' travellers passing through or near Sherwood Forest to 'come to dinner'. Then the guests were asked how much money they could pay – if they answered honestly they were sent on their way. If not, the merry men took everything they had. When the Sheriff of Nottingham was Robin Hood's guest, they really did take everything – the Sheriff left the forest with only his underwear.

HARDOMETER

CUNNING: 8
COURAGE: 9
SURVIVAL SKILLS: 8
RUTHLESSNESS: 7

ARCHERY CONTEST

In one story, the Sheriff of Nottingham organised an archery competition hoping to get Robin Hood (who was famous for his amazing archery skills) to come out of hiding. Robin Hood couldn't resist entering the contest in disguise. He won the competition (of course), but was captured by the Sheriff and had to be rescued by his merry men, who included the enormous Little John, young Much the Miller's son, red-silk wearing Will Scarlett, and happy Friar Tuck.

THE REAL ROBIN HOOD

The earliest stories about Robin Hood date from the 1100s, but they weren't written down. Over the centuries, tales have been added to and changed, and new stories and films are made about Robin Hood all the time. Robin Hood might even have been a real person who lived in Nottinghamshire or Yorkshire, living as an outlaw and defying authority.

YOU CAN KEEP THOSE!

THESEUS

**Theseus is the hard nut
minotaur-bashing hero
of Greek legend.**

PRINCE THESEUS

Theseus was really the son of the King of Athens, but he
didn't find out until he was a young man. His mother told him
to lift up a rock, where he found sandals and a sword that
his father had left for him, to make the journey to Athens.

THE ROAD TO ATHENS

Theseus' trip to Athens was beset by evil murderers: one
catapulted travellers from pine trees, another fed them to
a man-eating turtle, while another offered a bed for the
night that was either too long or too short, then cut the
travellers to fit! Theseus gave all the
baddies a taste of their own medicine.

PROBLEMS IN ATHENS

When Theseus arrived in Athens, his father, King Aegeus, recognised him from the sword and sandals only after Theseus narrowly avoided being poisoned by his step-mother, Medea (see page 32). Athens had a problem: every nine years, seven Athenian boys and girls had to be sent to King Minos of Crete, where they were fed to a bull-headed monster, the Minotaur, who lived in a labyrinth. King Aegeus asked Theseus to solve the problem.

THESEUS AND THE MINOTAUR

Theseus travelled to Athens with the sacrificial Athenian children. With the help of the King of Crete's daughter, Ariadne, who gave him a magic thread to help him find his way out of the maze, he killed the monstrous Minotaur with his bare hands, saving the children of Athens from a dreadful fate, and sailed off with Ariadne.

UNHAPPY ENDINGS

Theseus had promised his father that he'd hoist white sails from his ship if his mission had been successful, but he forgot to change the ship's black sails. King Aegeus was waiting anxiously in Athens for a glimpse of the ship. He saw the black sails and assumed Theseus was dead. Since the whole minotaur-killing plan had been his idea, Aegeus threw himself into the sea and drowned. Theseus became king of Athens, and had other adventures, but he's most famous for his minotaur-bashing. Theseus died when he was pushed off a cliff by the King of Skyros.

HARDOMETER

CUNNING: 7
COURAGE: 10
SURVIVAL SKILLS: 6
RUTHLESSNESS: 9

GREEK MYTHS

The Greek myths are full of fearless heroes like Heracles and Theseus (see pages 8 and 52), gods interfering in human lives and magic. But one of the best things about the Greek myths are the monsters. Here are a few of them:

Name: The Chimera
Appearance: Cross between a lion and a goat, with a snake for a tail.
Famous For: Breathing fire and terrorising the people of Lydia.
Dreadful Fate: Shot with an arrow by Bellerophon, riding Pegasus the flying horse.

Name: The Gorgons
Appearance: Women with snakes for hair.
Famous For: Turning anyone who looks at them to stone.
Dreadful Fate: One of the gorgons, Medusa, had her head chopped off by the hero Perseus, who looked at her reflection in a shield and avoided being turned to stone.

Name: The Harpies
Appearance: The head of a woman and the body of a bird.
Famous For: Carrying off people and objects. The harpies were sent to torment King Phineas, flying off with his food before he could eat it and pooing on the scraps that were left!
Dreadful Fate: Driven off by the sons of the north wind but not killed, the harpies live on in a cave on the island of Crete.

Name: The Cyclops
Appearance: Giants with a single eye in the middle of their foreheads.
Famous For: Either working for the blacksmith god Hephaestus in his forge, or herding sheep on their own island, where the Greek hero Odysseus and his crew became trapped.
Dreadful Fate: The Cyclops Polyphemus was tricked by Odysseus and blinded.

Name: The Sphinx
Appearance: The body of a lion, a woman's face, and an eagle's wings.
Famous For: The sphinx lurked on the road to Thebes, where she asked travellers a riddle – if they got the riddle wrong, the sphinx strangled and ate them.
Dreadful Fate: The sphinx's riddle was answered by Oedipus, and the sphinx threw herself off a cliff.

Name: The Echidna
Appearance: Half-lovely young woman, half-snake.
Famous For: Eating people; being the mother of lots of other monsters, including the Chimera, Cerberus (the three-headed guard dog of the underworld), the Nemean lion (see page 8) and the Sphinx.
Dreadful Fate: She was killed by a many-eyed monster called Argus.

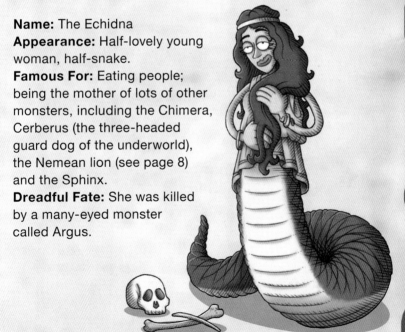

SIR GAWAIN

Sir Gawain is one of the greatest knights of King Arthur, the legendary British king.

HARD NUT RATING: 7.8

KNIGHTS OF THE ROUND TABLE

Sir Gawain is a model of knightly virtues: as well as being a rock-hard warrior, he's loyal to his king, courageous, and wise. There are more tales told about Sir Gawain than any other of King Arthur's Knights of the Round Table.

GREEN KNIGHT

The most famous story about Sir Gawain involves a terrifying Green Knight. One night, Gawain was sitting at the round table with King Arthur and the other knights, when a giant knight rode in on his horse. The knight was wearing green, carrying holly branches and (more worryingly) a huge axe. The mysterious knight issued a challenge: one of the men could chop off his head, but in a year's time the green knight would come back and chop off the head-chopper's head. Bravely, King Arthur said he would do it. Even more bravely, Sir Gawain stepped in to take his place. He chopped off the Green Knight's head, but the Green Knight calmly picked it up and walked out of the room.

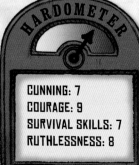

CUNNING: 7
COURAGE: 9
SURVIVAL SKILLS: 7
RUTHLESSNESS: 8

RETURN OF THE GREEN KNIGHT

Instead of hanging around waiting for the Green Knight to come back, Gawain set out to find him. On his journey, Gawain had to contend with wolves, dragons, ogres and enemy knights. One night, he stopped at the castle of Lord Bercilak, where Bercilak's wife flirted with Sir Gawain. Gawain was polite, but didn't flirt back, and eventually Bercilak's wife gave him a green sash, telling him it would protect him from harm. When they finally met, the Green Knight sliced at Gawain's head with his axe, but only grazed his neck. It turned out that Bercilak was really the Green Knight in disguise, and he spared Sir Gawain.

SIR GAWAIN'S FATE

An evil fairy called Morgan Le Faye had set up the trick, and was very disappointed when it didn't work. Her son, Mordred, was King Arthur's greatest enemy. In the final battle against Mordred, brave Sir Gawain died.

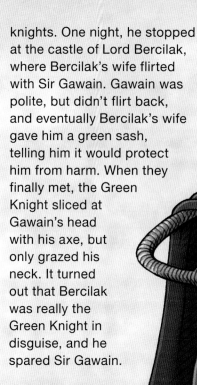

HARD NUT MYTHS AND LEGENDS TIMELINE

50,000 BC

The Aboriginal people first arrived in Australia. Their myths include stories about Thugine, the Rainbow Serpent.

3200 BC

The ancient Egyptian civilisation dates from around this time. They worshipped Re, the sun god, as well as lots of other gods and goddesses.

2750–2500 BC

Gilgamesh, King of Uruk lived around this time in ancient Sumeria. His story, involving monsters and a trip to the underworld, is one of the oldest stories ever written down.

1700

Hindu mythology was first written down around this time, including the story of the goddess Durga.

800–500 BC

The civilisation of ancient Greece dates from around this time. Ancient Greek myths include the stories of Medea, Heracles and Theseus.

19 BC

The Aeneid, a poem about the hero Aeneas whose descendants founded Rome, was written by Virgil, the ancient Roman poet.

AD 1

The stories of Cú Chulainn are set at about the beginning of the Christian era.

500

King Arthur, legendary British king, is supposed to have lived around this time.

500S

A poem telling the story of Chinese heroine Hua Mulan was first written down during this time.

700S-1100

The poem Beowulf, about a Swedish monster-killing hero, was written down some time during this period.

800

The Viking Age began around this date. The Vikings told stories of Thor, the thunder god, and many other gods, elves, dwarves, and giants.

1000

Stories about Clever Coyote were told in North America from around this time.

1100

Stories about Robin Hood, the outlaw who stole from the rich to give to the poor, date from the 1100s.

1100

The Boyhood Deeds of Finn, an Irish manuscript from around this date, tells the story of Finn McCool.

1300S-1600S

Fumo Liyongo, the Swahili poet, lived some time in this period. The real poet became mixed up with his stories of a super-strong hero.

1325

Tenochtitlan, the capital city of the Aztec Empire, was founded. As well as ruling an empire, the Aztecs worshipped and told stories about gods such as Quetzalcoatl, the feathered snake god.

1500S

The Chinese Monkey King first appeared in a novel written in the 1500s.

1900

Stories about Anansi, the African spider trickster, were first written down around this date, but they had been told for centuries.

GLOSSARY

AMAZONS Legendary race of big, strong female warriors

BANISHED Sent away from a place as a punishment

CASTANETS Musical instrument made of two wooden shells that click against each other

CHARIOT Horse-drawn vehicle often used in war

COMPASSIONATE Wanting to help others

CONTEND Deal with

DESTINY What will happen to someone in the future (fate)

DRUID Celtic priest, magician or educated person

EMBALM Preserve a dead body from decaying with special fluids or spices

EPIC POEM Long poem about a heroic person

FLIRT Playfully tease someone as if you are attracted to them

FRENZY Wild excitement or madness

GIRDLE Belt

IBIS Long-legged wading bird

IMMERSED Dipped in liquid

IMMORTAL Ability to live forever

INJUSTICE Unfairness

JACKAL Small wolf-like animal

LABYRINTH Maze

MAIZE Grain plant (corn)

MORTALLY WOUNDED Injured so seriously that it causes death

NAVEL Belly button

OPTIMISTIC Hopeful and confident about the future

OUTLAW Criminal who is outside the protection of the law

OUTWITTED Tricked, got the better of

PESSIMISTIC Believing that the worst will happen

PROPHESIED Stated that something will happen in the future

PYRE Pile of wood for burning a dead body on

RAMPAGING Moving through a place violently and uncontrollably

RIDDLE Puzzle

SACRIFICIAL Something to be killed

SCARAB Type of beetle worshipped by the ancient Egyptians

SCEPTRE Special staff or wand carried by a king or queen

STAMPEDE Crowd of animals running together in panic

TRIDENT Three-pronged spear

VORACIOUS Wanting or eating huge amounts of food

INDEX